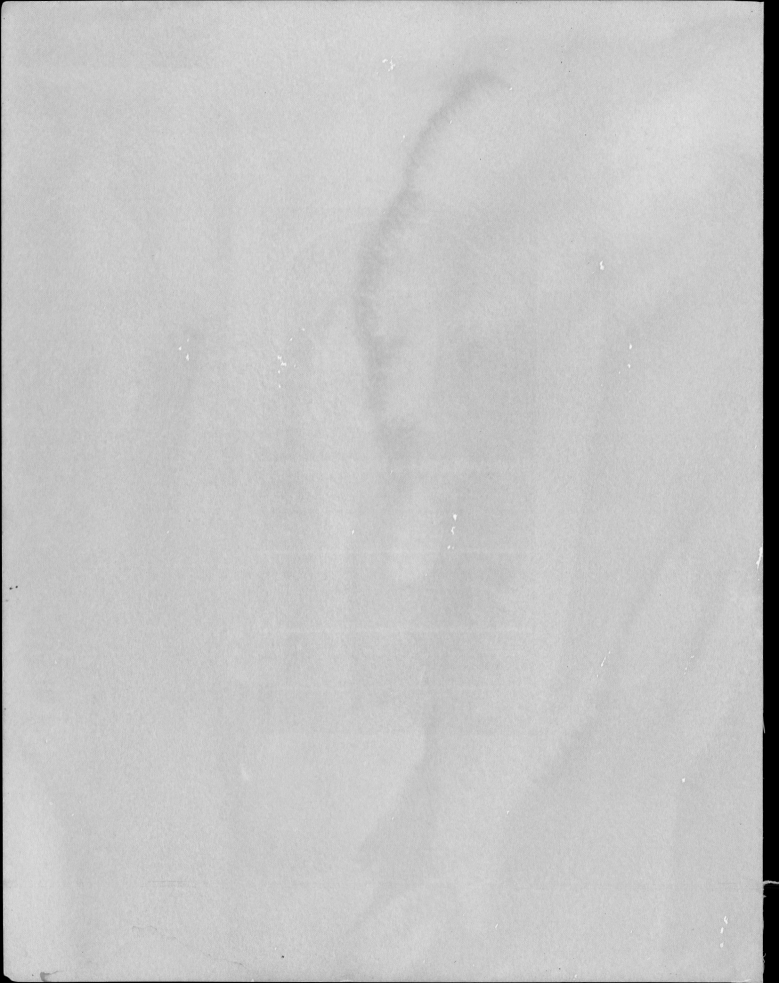

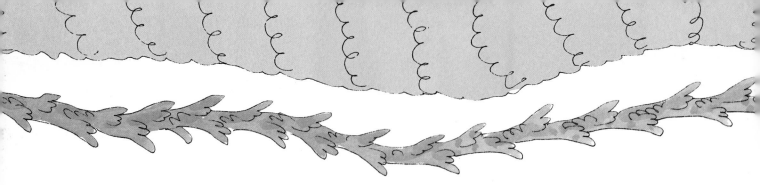

For my nephew Rory
C. V.

Copyright © 1991 by Charlotte Voake

All rights reserved.

First U.S. paperback edition 1996

The Library of Congress has cataloged the hardcover edition as follows:

Voake, Charlotte.
The three little pigs and other favorite nursery stories /
[adapted and] illustrated by Charlotte Voake.—1st U.S. ed.
Summary: Ten familiar children's stories including Henny Penny, Goldilocks, and Mr. Vinegar.
ISBN 1-56402-118-1 (hardcover)
1. Tales. [1. Folklore.] I. Three little pigs. II. Title.
PZ8.1.V56Th   1992
398.2—dc20
[E]   91-58759

ISBN 1-56402-957-3 (paperback)

2 4 6 8 10 9 7 5 3 1

Printed in Hong Kong

This book was typeset in Garamond.
The pictures were done in watercolor and ink.

Candlewick Press
2067 Massachusetts Avenue
Cambridge, Massachusetts 02140

The
THREE
LITTLE PIGS

AND OTHER
FAVORITE NURSERY STORIES

illustrated by
CHARLOTTE VOAKE

CANDLEWICK PRESS
CAMBRIDGE, MASSACHUSETTS

CONT

The Gingerbread Boy *8*

Lazy Jack *16*

The Three Billy Goats Gruff *24*

Henny Penny *32*

Goldilocks and the Three Bears *40*

ENTS

The Little Red Hen 48

Little Red Riding Hood 54

Mr. Vinegar 62

The Musicians of Bremen 72

The Three Little Pigs 82

THE GINGERBREAD BOY

Once upon a time a little old man and a little old woman lived together in a little old house. They had no children, so one day the little old woman made a boy out of gingerbread and put him in the oven to bake.

When the gingerbread boy was baked, the little old woman went to take him from the oven, but as soon as she opened the door, out jumped the gingerbread boy, and away he ran, across the kitchen, out of the little old house, and down the lane. "Stop! Stop!" cried the little old woman, running after the gingerbread boy; and "Stop! Stop!" cried the little old man, running after the little old woman.

But the gingerbread boy just laughed and shouted:
"Run, run, as fast as you can!
You can't catch me.
I'm the gingerbread man!"
And they couldn't catch him.

The gingerbread boy ran on and on
until he met
a cow.

"Stop! Stop!

little gingerbread boy!"

said the cow. "I want to eat you."

But the gingerbread boy just laughed and shouted:

"I have run away from a little old woman and a little

old man, and I can run away from you, I can, I can!

Run, run, as fast as you can!

You can't catch me.

I'm the gingerbread man!"

And the cow couldn't catch him.

The gingerbread boy
ran on and on
until he met a horse.
"Stop! Stop! little
gingerbread boy!" said
the horse. "I want to eat you."

But the gingerbread boy just laughed and shouted:

"I have run away from a little old woman and a little

old man and a cow, and I can run away from you,

I can, I can!

Run, run, as fast as you can!

You can't catch me.

I'm the gingerbread man!"

And the horse couldn't catch him.

The gingerbread boy ran on and on until he met

some farm workers cutting hay in a field.

"Stop! Stop! little gingerbread boy!" said the farm workers. "We want to eat you."

But the gingerbread boy just laughed and shouted:

"I have run away from a little old

woman and a little old man

and a cow and a horse,

and I can run away from you,

I can, I can!

Run, run, as fast as you can!

You can't catch me.

I'm the gingerbread man!"

And the farm workers couldn't catch him.

The gingerbread boy ran on and on

until he met a fox.

"Stop! Stop! little gingerbread boy!"

said the fox. "I want to eat you."

But the gingerbread boy just laughed and shouted:

"I have run away from a little old woman and a little old man and a cow and a horse and lots of farm workers, and I can run away from you, I can, I can!

Run, run, as fast as you can!

You can't catch me.

I'm the gingerbread man!"

"Oh yes, I can catch you," said the cunning fox. "You just wait and see."

The gingerbread boy ran on and on until he

came to a river, and there he had to stop.

Just then the fox came up beside him.

"Jump on my tail, little gingerbread boy," said the fox. "I'll be happy to take you across."

So the gingerbread boy jumped on the fox's tail, and the fox began to swim across the river.

When he was a little way into the water, the fox turned his head and said, "You are too heavy for my tail, little gingerbread boy, and I fear you may get wet. Jump on my back instead."

So the gingerbread boy jumped on the fox's back.

In the middle of the river, the fox turned his head again and said, "I fear you may get wet on my back, little gingerbread boy. Jump on my head instead."

So the gingerbread boy jumped on the fox's head.

When they were almost across the river, the fox said, "You are growing too heavy for my head, little gingerbread boy. Jump on my nose instead."

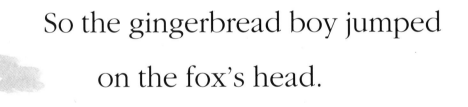

So the gingerbread boy jumped on the fox's nose.

As soon as the fox reached the far shore of the river, he threw back his head with a sudden *snip-snap!*

"Oh dear, oh dear!" said the gingerbread boy. "I'm afraid I am a quarter gone!"

Crunch, munch, went the fox.

"Oh, goodness me!" said the gingerbread boy.

"I'm afraid I am three-quarters gone!"

Crunch, munch, swallow,

went the fox.

And the gingerbread boy never spoke another word.

LAZY JACK

Once upon a time there was a boy whose name was Jack, and he lived with his mother in the country. They were very poor, and the old lady made her living by spinning. But Jack was so lazy that he did nothing but bask in the sun in the summer and sit by the fire in the winter. So everyone called him Lazy Jack.

At last, one Monday, Jack's mother told him
she would turn him out of the house if he
did not begin to work for his porridge.
So the next day Jack went out and
hired himself to a farmer for a penny.
But as he was coming home, never
having had any money before,
he dropped the penny in a stream.

"Oh, you silly boy," said his mother, "you should
have put the money in your pocket."

"I'll do so another time," replied Jack.

On Wednesday Jack went out again
and hired himself to a cow-keeper, who
gave him a jar of milk for his day's work.

Jack put the jar into the large pocket of
his jacket, spilling it all long before he got home.

"Dear me," said his mother, "you should have carried it on your head."

"I'll do so another time," replied Jack.

On Thursday Jack hired himself again to a farmer, who agreed to give him a cream cheese for his services. In the evening Jack walked home with the cheese on his head. By the time he got home, the cheese was spoiled, part of it being lost, and part matted with his hair.

"Oh no, Jack," said his mother, "you should have carried it carefully in your hands."

"I'll do so another time," replied Jack.

On Friday Jack hired himself to a baker, who would give him nothing for his work but a large tomcat. Jack took the cat and began carrying it carefully in his hands, but in a short time, Pussy scratched him so much that he had to let it go. When he got home, his mother said, "Oh, for goodness' sake, Jack, you should have led it home on a string."

"I'll do so another time," replied Jack. On Saturday Jack hired himself to a butcher, who gave him a shoulder of mutton for his work. So Jack tied the mutton to a string and dragged it after him in the dirt. By the time Jack got home, the meat was completely spoiled. This time his mother was quite out of patience with him, for the next day was Sunday and all she had for dinner was cabbage. "You ninny-hammer," she said, "you should have carried it on your shoulder."

"I'll do so another time," replied Jack.

The next Monday Jack hired himself to a cattle-keeper, who gave him a donkey for his trouble. Jack found it hard to lift the donkey onto his shoulder, but at last he did so and began walking slowly home.

Now it happened that on the way he passed the house of a rich man, whose only daughter was very beautiful, but deaf and dumb. This girl had never laughed in her life, and only laughter could cure her, so her doctor said. As luck would have it, she was looking out of her window when Jack passed by carrying the donkey. The sight was so strange she burst into a great fit of laughter and immediately recovered her speech and hearing.

The rich man was overjoyed and so was she, and in next to no time, Lazy Jack and the beautiful girl were married.

They lived in a large house and had all they ever
needed, and Jack's mother lived with them
in great happiness until she died.

THE THREE BILLY GOATS GRUFF

Once upon a time three billy goats lived
together in a field on a hillside.

Their names were  Big Billy Goat Gruff,

Middle Billy Goat Gruff,

and Little Billy Goat Gruff.

A river ran beside the billy goats' field, and one day they decided to cross it and eat the grass on the other side. But first they had to go over the bridge, and under the bridge lived a great ugly Troll.

First Little Billy Goat Gruff stepped onto
the bridge.

   TRIP TRAP,

went his hooves.

"Who's that tripping over my bridge?"

roared the Troll.

"It is only I, Little Billy Goat Gruff, going across

the river to make myself fat,"

said Little Billy Goat Gruff in

such a small

voice.

"Now I'm coming to
gobble you up," said the Troll.

"Oh, please don't eat me. I'm so small," said Little

Billy Goat Gruff. "Wait for the next billy goat.

He's much bigger."

"Well, be off with you," said the Troll.

A little while later, Middle Billy Goat Gruff

stepped onto the bridge.

TRIP TRAP, TRIP TRAP,

went his hooves.

"Who's that tripping over my

bridge?" roared the Troll.

"It is only I, Middle Billy Goat Gruff, going across

the river to make myself fat," said Middle

Billy Goat Gruff, whose voice was

not so small.

"Now I'm coming to gobble

you up," said the Troll.

"Oh, no, don't eat me," said Middle Billy Goat

Gruff. "Wait for the next billy goat. He's the

biggest of all."

"Very well, be off with you," said the Troll.

It wasn't long before Big Billy Goat Gruff stepped onto the bridge. *TRIP TRAP, TRIP TRAP, TRIP TRAP*, went his hooves, and the bridge groaned under his weight.

"Who's that tramping over my bridge?" roared the Troll.

"It is I, Big Billy Goat Gruff," said Big Billy Goat Gruff, who had a rough, roaring voice of his own. "Now I'm coming to gobble you up," said the Troll, and at once he jumped onto the bridge, immensely horrible and hungry.

But Big Billy Goat Gruff was
very fierce and strong. He put
down his head and charged the Troll
and butted him so hard he flew high into
the air and then fell down, down, down, *splash*
into the middle of the river. And the great ugly
Troll was never seen again.

Then Big Billy Goat Gruff joined Middle Billy Goat Gruff and Little Billy Goat Gruff in the field on the far side of the river. There they got so fat that they could hardly walk home again, and if the fat hasn't fallen off them, they're still fat now.

So *snip, snap, snout,* this tale's told out!

HENNY PENNY

One day Henny Penny was scratching around in the farmyard when *whack!* an acorn hit her on the head. "Goodness gracious me!" said Henny Penny. "The sky's a-going to fall. I must go and tell the king."

She went along and she went along and she went

along, and soon she met Cocky Locky.

"Where are you going?"

asked Cocky Locky.

"I'm going to tell

the king the sky's a-falling," said Henny Penny.

"May I come with you?" asked Cocky Locky.

"Certainly," said Henny Penny.

So they both went to tell the king the sky was falling.

They went along and they went along and they

went along, and soon they met Ducky Daddles.

"Where are you going?" asked Ducky Daddles.

"We're going to tell the king

the sky's a-falling,"

said Henny Penny

and Cocky Locky.

"May I come with you?" asked Ducky Daddles.

"Certainly," said Henny Penny and Cocky Locky.

So they all went to tell the king the sky was falling.

They went along and they went along and they went along, and soon they met Goosey Poosey.

"Where are you going?" asked Goosey Poosey.

"We're going to tell the king the sky's a-falling," said Henny Penny, Cocky Locky, and Ducky Daddles.

"May I come with you?" asked Goosey Poosey.

"Certainly," said Henny Penny, Cocky Locky, and Ducky Daddles.

So they all went to tell the king the sky was falling.

They went along and they went along and they

went along, and soon they met Turkey Lurkey.

"Where are you going?" asked Turkey Lurkey.

"We're going to tell the king the

sky's a-falling," said Henny Penny,

Cocky Locky, Ducky Daddles, and Goosey Poosey.

"May I come with you?" asked Turkey Lurkey.

"Certainly," said Henny Penny, Cocky Locky,

Ducky Daddles, and Goosey Poosey.

So they all went to tell the king the sky was falling.

They went along and they went along and they

went along, and soon they met Foxy Woxy.

"Where are you going?" asked Foxy Woxy.

"We're going to tell the king

the sky's a-falling,"

said Henny Penny, Cocky Locky,

Ducky Daddles, Goosey Poosey, and Turkey Lurkey.

"But this is not the way to the king,"
said Foxy Woxy. "I know the right
way. Let me show you."
"Oh, certainly," said
Henny Penny, Cocky Locky, Ducky Daddles,
Goosey Poosey, and Turkey Lurkey.

So they all went
with Foxy Woxy to tell
the king the sky was falling.
They went along and they went along
and they went along, and soon they
came to a dark and narrow hole.

Now this was the door of Foxy Woxy's home, but Foxy Woxy said, "This is a shortcut to the king's palace. I will go in first, and you come after."

"Why, of course, certainly, without a doubt, why not?" said Henny Penny, Cocky Locky, Ducky Daddles, Goosey Poosey, and Turkey Lurkey.

So Foxy Woxy went along a little way, and then turned around to wait.

Turkey Lurkey came first into the dark and narrow hole.

Hrumph! Snap!

Foxy Woxy bit off Turkey Lurkey's head. Next Goosey Poosey came into the dark and narrow hole.

Hrumph! Snap! Foxy Woxy bit off Goosey Poosey's head. Next Ducky Daddles waddled into the dark and narrow hole. *Hrumph! Snap!* Foxy Woxy bit off Ducky Daddles's head. Next Cocky Locky strutted into the dark and narrow hole.

Hrumph! Snap! Foxy Woxy tried to bite off Cocky Locky's head, but he missed. Cocky Locky called out to Henny Penny, then *Hrumph! Snap!* Foxy Woxy tried again, and this time he did bite off Cocky Locky's head.

Henny Penny heard Cocky Locky's call, and she turned tail and ran home as fast as she could.

So she never told the king the sky was falling.

GOLDILOCKS

and
THE THREE BEARS

Once upon a time there were three bears—Daddy Bear, Mommy Bear, and little Baby Bear. They all lived together in a cottage in the woods. Every morning the three bears had porridge for breakfast. They each had their own bowl—a great big bowl for Daddy Bear, a medium-sized bowl for Mommy Bear, and a little baby bowl for little Baby Bear. One morning they sat down to eat their porridge and found that it was too hot.

"Let's go for a walk in the woods," said Mommy Bear. "When we get back, our porridge will be cool enough to eat."

No sooner had the three bears gone out than a little girl with golden hair came up to the cottage. Her name was Goldilocks. She pushed open the door and walked straight in.

"Oh! Lovely porridge! My favorite!" she said.

First Goldilocks tasted the porridge in the great big bowl. "Much too hot!" she said.

Next she tasted the porridge in the medium-sized bowl.

"Much too salty!" she said.

Last she tasted the porridge in the little baby bowl. "Just exactly right!" she said and ate it all up, every bit.

"Now," said Goldilocks, looking around the room, "I will try one of these chairs."

First she sat on the great big chair. "Much too hard!" she said.

Next she sat on the medium-sized chair. "Much too soft!" she said.

Last she sat on the little baby chair.

"Just exactly right!" she said. But then *crack!*

splinter! crash!—the chair broke all to pieces.

"Now," said Goldilocks, "I will go and lie down, because I do feel very tired."

She went upstairs to the three bears' bedroom.

"Oh! Oh! Oh!" she said. "Three lovely beds to choose from!" First she tried the great big bed.

"Much too high!" she said.

Next she tried the medium-sized bed.

"Much too lumpy!" she said.

Last she tried the little baby bed. "Just exactly right!" she said, and she got right in and pulled up the covers, and soon she was fast asleep.

Before long the three bears came back from their walk. They were all very hungry. Daddy Bear looked at his great big bowl.

"Someone's been eating my porridge!" he said in a great big voice. Mommy Bear looked at her medium-sized bowl.

"Someone's been eating my porridge!" she said in a medium-sized voice. Then little Baby Bear looked at his little baby bowl and said, "Someone's been eating my porridge and has EATEN IT ALL UP!"

"Look at this!" Daddy Bear said in a great big voice. "Someone's been sitting on my chair!"

"Someone's been sitting on my chair, too," said Mommy Bear in a medium-sized voice.

"And someone's been sitting on my chair," said little Baby Bear in a little baby voice, "and they've BROKEN IT ALL TO BITS!" The three bears ran upstairs.

"Someone's been lying on my bed," Daddy Bear said in a great big voice.

"Someone's been lying on my bed, too,"

Mommy Bear said in a medium-sized voice.

"And someone's been lying on my bed,"

said little Baby Bear in a little baby voice,

"and SHE'S STILL HERE!"

Goldilocks woke up and saw

the three bears all looking

down at her.

So she leapt out of bed, ran across
the room, and jumped
straight out of the window.
Then she ran home as fast
as she possibly could.
And the three bears
never saw her again.

THE LITTLE RED HEN

Once upon a time there was a little red hen who lived on a farm with a dog, a goose, and a cat.

One day the little red hen was scratching around in the farmyard when she found some grains of wheat.

"Who will help me plant this wheat?" she asked.

"I'm busy," said the dog.

"So am I," said the cat.

"So am I," said the goose.

I'm busy

"Then I shall plant it myself," she said.

And she did.

Every day the little red hen watered the ground, until tiny shoots appeared and the wheat began to grow. She watched it and weeded it, and slowly it grew tall and strong. Then one day the little red hen saw that the wheat was ready for cutting.

"Who will help me cut the wheat?" she asked.

"I'm busy," said the cat.

"So am I," said the dog.

"So am I," said the goose.

"Then I'll cut it myself," she said. And she did.

Once the wheat was cut, it had to be threshed, and the grain put into a sack.

"Who will help me thresh the wheat?" asked the little red hen.

"I'm busy," said the dog.

"So am I," said the cat.

"So am I," said the goose.

"Then I'll thresh it myself," she said. And she did.

Now the wheat was ready to be taken to the mill,  to be ground into flour.

"Who will help me take the wheat to the mill?" asked the little red hen.

"It's too far," said the dog.

"Much too far," said the cat.

"Far too far," said the goose.

"Then I'll take it myself," she said. And she did.

The miller ground the wheat into flour, and the

little red hen brought the flour back home.

Now it was time for baking.

"Who will help me bake the bread?"

asked the little red hen.

"Not I," said the cat.

"Not I," said the goose.

"Not I," said the dog.

"Then I'll bake it myself," she said. And she did.

When the bread came out of the oven, it smelled

so good that the dog and the cat and the goose

came running.

The little red hen cut it into thick, delicious slices.

"This bread is ready to be eaten," she said,

"and who will help me eat it?"

"I will," said the dog.

"I will," said the cat.

"I will," said

the goose.

I WILL!

"Oh, no you won't!" said the little red hen,
and she ate it all
up herself.

LITTLE RED RIDING HOOD

Once upon a time there was a little girl who lived with her mother at the edge of a forest. Her grandmother, who loved her very much, had made her a red cloak with a hood, and she wore it so often that everyone called her Little Red Riding Hood.

One day her mother said to her, "Your grandma is ill and all alone in her cottage in the forest, and I want you to take her this basket

of cakes. Make sure you don't talk to any
strangers on the way."

Little Red Riding Hood set off on the path, and
she had not gone very far before she met a wolf.

"Good morning," said the wolf. "Where are you going in your beautiful red cloak?"

"I'm taking this basket of cakes to my grandma, who is ill in bed," Little Red Riding Hood replied.

"Where does your grandma live?" asked the wolf.

"In the cottage at the end of the path," said Little Red Riding Hood.

Now the wolf was very hungry, and he wanted to eat Little Red Riding Hood there and then. But he

heard a woodcutter working near-by, so he ran off. The wolf went straight through the forest to the grandmother's cottage and knocked at her door, *rat-tat-tat*.

"Who's there?" Grandma called.

"It's Little Red Riding Hood, and I've brought you

a basket of cakes," said the wolf, in as girlish a voice as he could.

"Then lift the latch and let yourself in," said Grandma.

The wolf lifted the latch and bounded in and swallowed her in one gulp. Then he put on her shawl and nightcap and climbed into her bed. Before long Little Red Riding Hood came to the cottage and knocked at the door, *rat-tat-tat*.

"Who's there?" asked the wolf in a croaky voice.

"It's me, Grandma, and I've brought you a basket of cakes," said Little Red Riding Hood.

"Then lift the latch and let yourself in," said the wolf, pulling the quilt up to his chin.

Little Red Riding Hood lifted the latch and walked into the cottage.

"Why, Grandma, what big eyes you've got."

"All the better to see you with, my dear,"

said the wolf.

"And, Grandma, what big ears you've got."

"All the better to hear you with, my dear,"

said the wolf.

"And, Grandma, what big teeth you've got."

"All the better to eat you with!" growled the wolf,

and he jumped
out of bed and
ate Little Red
Riding Hood.

Just then the woodcutter came by
the cottage and noticed that the door was open,
so he looked inside.

And when he saw the wolf licking his chops, he
cut off the wolf's head with his ax.

Then Little Red Riding Hood and her grandma
stepped out from inside the wolf,
and from that day on
Little Red Riding Hood
never, ever talked
to strangers
again.

MR. VINEGAR

Mr. and Mrs. Vinegar lived in a vinegar bottle. Now one day, when Mr. Vinegar was out, Mrs. Vinegar was busy sweeping and an unlucky thump of the broom brought the whole house *clitter-clatter, clitter-clatter,* around her ears. She rushed out to find her husband and cried out, on seeing him,

"Mr. Vinegar, Mr. Vinegar, we are ruined, we are ruined! I have knocked the house down, and it is all in pieces!"

Then Mr. Vinegar said, "My dear, let us see what can be done.

Here is the door. I will take it on my back, and we will go forth to seek our fortune."

Mr. and Mrs. Vinegar walked all day and at nightfall entered a forest. They were both very tired, and Mr. Vinegar said,

"My love, I will climb up into a tree, drag up the door, and you follow." Which they did, and stretched out on the door, and soon fell fast asleep. In the middle of the night they were woken by voices beneath the tree and found that a band of thieves had gathered there to divide their booty. "Here, Jack," said one thief, "here are five coins for you; here, Bill, here are ten coins for you; here, Bob, here are three coins for you."

Mr. and Mrs. Vinegar trembled and trembled so much with fear that the door fell out of the tree, and though the thieves scampered away, Mr. and Mrs. Vinegar hung onto a branch all night, and only dared come down in the morning. When Mr. Vinegar went to lift up the door, what did he find under it but a number of gold coins.

"Mrs. Vinegar, Mrs. Vinegar," he cried, "our fortune is made, our fortune is made!" Mrs. Vinegar jumped for joy when she saw the money. "My dear," she said, "I'll tell you what to do. Go to the nearest town and buy a cow. I can make butter and cheese, which you shall sell at market, and we'll both live happily ever after."

So Mr. Vinegar took the money and went to the nearest town. When he arrived, he walked up and down and up and down and at last saw a beautiful red cow. Oh, he thought, if I could have that cow I'd be the happiest man alive. So he offered all his money for the cow, and the owner, most obligingly, sold it to him. Then Mr. Vinegar walked up and down and up and down with his cow, to show everyone how happy he was. By and by he saw a man playing the bagpipes, *tweedle-dum, tweedle-dee*. Children were following the man wherever he went, and he appeared to be pocketing money on all sides. Oh, thought Mr. Vinegar, if I could have those bagpipes

I'd be the happiest man alive. So Mr. Vinegar spoke to the man, and the man said, most obligingly, he could have the bagpipes in exchange for the cow. "Done!" said Mr. Vinegar in great delight. Then he walked up and down and up and down with his

bagpipes, but it was in vain he tried to play a tune and instead of pocketing money on all sides, he only made the children hoot and laugh and pelt him with all sorts of rubbish. Poor Mr. Vinegar, his fingers grew very cold, and just as he was leaving the town, he met a man wearing a fine thick pair of gloves. Oh, thought Mr. Vinegar, if I could have those gloves I'd be the happiest man alive. So he went up to the man, and told him how much he liked the gloves, and the man, most obligingly, agreed to give him the gloves in exchange for the bagpipes, which made Mr. Vinegar perfectly happy as he trudged on toward home. But it was a long, long way, and it had been a long, long day, and Mr. Vinegar grew very tired. And when he passed a man with a good stout walking stick, oh, thought Mr. Vinegar, if I could have that walking stick I'd be the happiest man alive. So he spoke to the man, and after much discussion the man agreed, most obligingly, that Mr. Vinegar could have the stick if he could have the gloves. And Mr. Vinegar, because his hands were so warm, was happy to make the exchange.

As Mr. Vinegar drew near the place where he had left his wife, he heard a parrot on a tree calling out his name.

"Mr. Vinegar, Mr. Vinegar, you foolish man, you blockhead, you simpleton! You went to the market and gave all your money for a cow. Then you gave away the cow for bagpipes, which you could not play. Then you gave away the bagpipes for a pair of gloves. Then you gave away the gloves for a poor miserable stick, which you could have found in any hedge."

Then the parrot laughed and laughed and laughed.
Mr. Vinegar fell into a violent rage and threw the
stick at the parrot's head. The stick stuck in the tree.
So in the end Mr. Vinegar came back to Mrs. Vinegar
without money, cow, bagpipes, gloves, or stick, and
she instantly chased him off and away
and they have never ever
been seen
again.

THE MUSICIANS OF BREMEN

There was once a donkey who decided to go to the town of Bremen to become a musician.

On his way he met a dog, who was sitting by the roadside looking miserable.

"What's the matter with you, Dog?" asked the donkey.

"Nobody loves me, and I don't have anything to do," said the dog.

"Come with me to Bremen, and you can be a musician,"

said the donkey. "I'll play the guitar and you can play the drums."

So on they went together along the road to Bremen. They had not gone far before they met a cat, sitting on its own looking as sad as can be.

"What's the matter with you, Cat?" asked the donkey.

"Nobody loves me, and I don't have anything to do," said the cat.

"Come with us to Bremen, and you can be a musician," said the donkey. "I'll play the guitar, Dog will play the drums, and you can play the violin."

So on they went together along the road to Bremen.

A mile or two

further on they

met a rooster perched droopily on a gatepost. "What's the matter with you, Rooster?" asked the donkey.

"Nobody loves me, and I don't have anything to do," said the rooster.

"Come with us to Bremen, and you can be a musician," said the donkey. "I'll play the guitar, Dog will play the drums, Cat will play the violin, and you can be the singer."

So on they went together along the road to Bremen. It was a long way to Bremen, and they still had not gotten there when night

began to fall. So they needed somewhere to stay.
As they were passing through the woods, Rooster
saw a light in the distance, and when they came
closer it turned out to be shining from a little
cottage. Before knocking at the door, they
decided first to peep through the window.
The donkey put his hooves up on the
windowsill and looked in.
"What can you see?"
asked Rooster.
"Food, lots of
food," said the
donkey.
"And what else?"
asked Cat.
"Chairs, comfortable chairs,"

said the donkey. "And what else?" asked Dog.

"Fire, a lovely warm fire," said the donkey.

"And what else?" asked all three together.

"Four robbers eating their dinner," said the donkey and ran with the others back into the woods. What the animals needed now was a plan, and it didn't take them long to make one.

Very quietly they came back to the cottage.

The donkey put his hooves on the windowsill, Dog jumped onto Donkey's back, Cat jumped onto Dog's back, and Rooster jumped onto Cat's head. Then all together they began to make music.

Ee-aw, ee-aw, bow-wow-wow,

miaow, miaow, cock-a-doodle-doo!

And they fell into the room through the window,

with the glass smashing

all around them.

The robbers were so frightened,

they ran out of the cottage and into the woods.

Now it was the animals' turn to be warm and full of food and as comfortable as could be.

The animals settled down for the night. The donkey found a perfect pile of straw in the yard, Dog lay behind the door, Cat curled up by the fire, and Rooster flew up into the rafters. Soon they were fast asleep.

When the light went out in the cottage, one of the robbers came back to find out what was going on. He crept into the room and tried to light a match from what he thought were the embers of the fire. But he was wrong. These were the fiery

eyes of Cat, and Cat leapt at him, hissing and scratching. He stepped back and fell over Dog, who bit him in the leg.

He ran into the yard, where Donkey gave him a great kick. Finally Rooster, disturbed by the noise, crowed out, *Cock-a-doodle-doo!*

The robber ran in terror to his friends in the woods. "There's a terrible witch in the house," he cried, "who leapt up and scratched my face. And by the door there's a man with a knife, who stabbed me in the leg. And in the yard there's a great black monster, who beat me with a club. And on the roof there's a judge, who shouted, 'I'll lock you up, you rascal, you!'"

So the robbers never went near the cottage again. As for Donkey, Dog, Cat, and Rooster, they never got to Bremen but lived happily ever after in the cottage in the woods, making a great deal of noise when they felt like it.

THE THREE LITTLE PIGS

Once upon a time there was an old mother pig with three little pigs, and since she was too poor to keep them, she sent them out to seek their fortune.

The first little pig set off, and he met a man with a bundle of straw. "Please, Man," said the pig, "give me that straw to build a house," which the man did, and the little pig built his house. Then along came a wolf and knocked at the door and said, "Little pig, little pig, let me come in." The little pig answered, "No, no, by the hair of my chinny chin chin!" So the wolf said, "Then I'll huff and I'll puff and I'll blow your house in." And the wolf huffed and he puffed and he blew the house in, and he ate up the first little pig.

The second little pig met a man with a bundle of sticks.

"Please, Man," said the pig, "give me those sticks to build a house," which the man did, and the second little pig built his house.

Then along came the wolf and knocked at the door and said, "Little pig, little pig, let me come in."

The little pig answered, "No, no, by the hair of my chinny chin chin!"

So the wolf said, "Then I'll huff and I'll puff and I'll blow your house in."

And the wolf huffed and he puffed, and he puffed and he huffed, and at last he blew the house in, and he ate up the second little pig.

The third little pig met a man with a load of bricks.

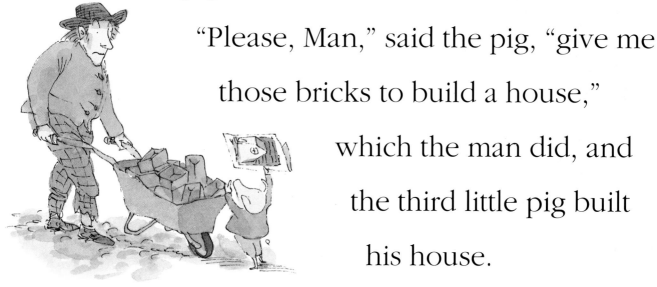

"Please, Man," said the pig, "give me those bricks to build a house," which the man did, and the third little pig built his house.

Then along came the wolf and knocked at the door and said, "Little pig, little pig, let me come in." The little pig answered, "No, no, by the hair of my chinny chin chin!" So the wolf said, "Then I'll huff and I'll puff and I'll blow your house in." And the wolf huffed and he puffed, and he puffed and he huffed, and he huffed and he puffed, but he could not blow the house in.

When the wolf found that he could not, with all his huffing and puffing, blow the house down, he said, "Little pig, I know where there is a nice field of turnips."

"Where?" said the little pig.

"Oh, in Mr. Smith's field, and if you will be ready tomorrow morning at six o'clock, I will call for you, and we will go together and get some dinner."

Well, the little pig got up at five o'clock and got the turnips before the wolf came. The wolf arrived at six and said, "Are you ready, little pig?"

"Ready!" replied the little pig. "I have already been and come back again and have a fine potful of turnips for dinner." The wolf was very angry, but he was determined to catch the little pig somehow, so he said, "Little pig, I know where there is a nice apple tree."

"Where?" said the little pig.

"Down at Merry Garden," replied the wolf. "I will come for you tomorrow at five o'clock, and we will go there together."

Well, the little pig got up at four o'clock and went off to get the apples, but it was a long way to go, and he had to climb the tree, and just as he was coming down, along came the wolf.

"Little pig, what! Are you here before me?" said the wolf. "And are they nice apples?"

"Yes, very," said the little pig. "I will throw one down to you."

And he threw it so far, that while the wolf was
fetching it, the little pig jumped down and ran home.
The next day the wolf came again and said to the
little pig, "Little pig, there is a fair at Shanklin
this afternoon, will you go?"

"Oh yes," said the pig, "I will go.
What time will you be ready?"

"At three," said
the wolf.

At two o'clock the little pig went to the fair and bought a butter churn. But on his way home, he saw the wolf coming, so he climbed into the churn to hide. But then the churn fell over and began to roll downhill, and it rolled right past the wolf.

And the wolf was so frightened, he ran home and never went to the fair at all.

Then the wolf went again to the little pig's house, and told the little pig how frightened he had been by a great round thing which rolled past him on the way to the fair.

"Hah!" said the little pig. "That was me! I had been to the fair and bought a butter churn, and when I saw you, I got into it and rolled down the hill."

Then the wolf was very angry indeed and said he would eat up the little pig, and he would come down the chimney to get him. So the little pig made a blazing fire, and put a huge pot of water to boil on it. Just as the wolf was coming down the chimney, the little pig took the lid off the pot, and in fell the wolf. So the little pig put on the lid again, boiled up the wolf until nothing was left of him, and lived happily ever after.

CHARLOTTE VOAKE says that the traditional nature of this book called for a straightforward approach to the artwork. "I wanted a certain lightness in the pictures as well, which made the artwork especially challenging," she explains. Charlotte Voake has illustrated many books for children, including *Over the Moon*, a collection of nursery rhymes, *Caterpillar Caterpillar* by Vivian French, and her own story *Mr. Davies and the Baby*.